Pippa
and
Poppa

First published in 2000
This edition published 2001 by
Franklin Watts
96 Leonard Street
London
EC2A 4XD

Franklin Watts Australia
56 O'Riordan Street
Alexandria
NSW 2015

A CIP catalogue record for this book is available
from the British Library.

ISBN 0 7496 3726 9 (hbk)
ISBN 0 7496 4386 2 (pbk)

Series Editor: Louise John
Series Advisor: Dr Barrie Wade
Series Designer: Jason Anscomb

Printed in Hong Kong

For Doll Reynolds and Pippa – A.C

Pippa
and
Poppa

by Anne Cassidy

Illustrated by Philip Norman

W

FRANKLIN WATTS

NEW YORK•LONDON•SYDNEY

When Granny went out
for the day, Pippa stayed
with Mum and Ben.

"Look after Pippa,"
Granny said.

"She is very precious."

Pippa was sad. She looked
for Granny in the garden ...

in the kitchen ...

and out of the window.

Ben felt sorry for Pippa.

He took her into the
garden to play football.

"Oh, no!" shouted Ben.

"Pippa has escaped."

Mum and Ben looked for
Pippa in the street.

Then they knocked on all
the doors.

"Granny will be very upset," said Mum.

"Pippa is very precious."

"Let's go to the Dog's Home," said Ben.

"Maybe someone will have found Pippa."

At the Dog's Home, Ruby showed them round.

Ben couldn't see Pippa
anywhere.

"We found this little dog last week," said Ruby.

"His name is Poppa."

"I've got an idea!" said Ben.

Mum, Ben and Ruby had
to get Poppa ready.

Mum and Ben took Poppa
to Granny's house.

Granny looked surprised.

"But Pippa is here!"
said Granny.

"She was waiting for me when I got home."

Now Granny has two dogs,
Pippa **and** Poppa.

They are both very precious.

Leapfrog has been specially designed to fit the requirements of the National Literacy Strategy. It offers real books for beginning readers by top authors and illustrators.

There are 25 Leapfrog stories to choose from: